INCORRECT
EYES

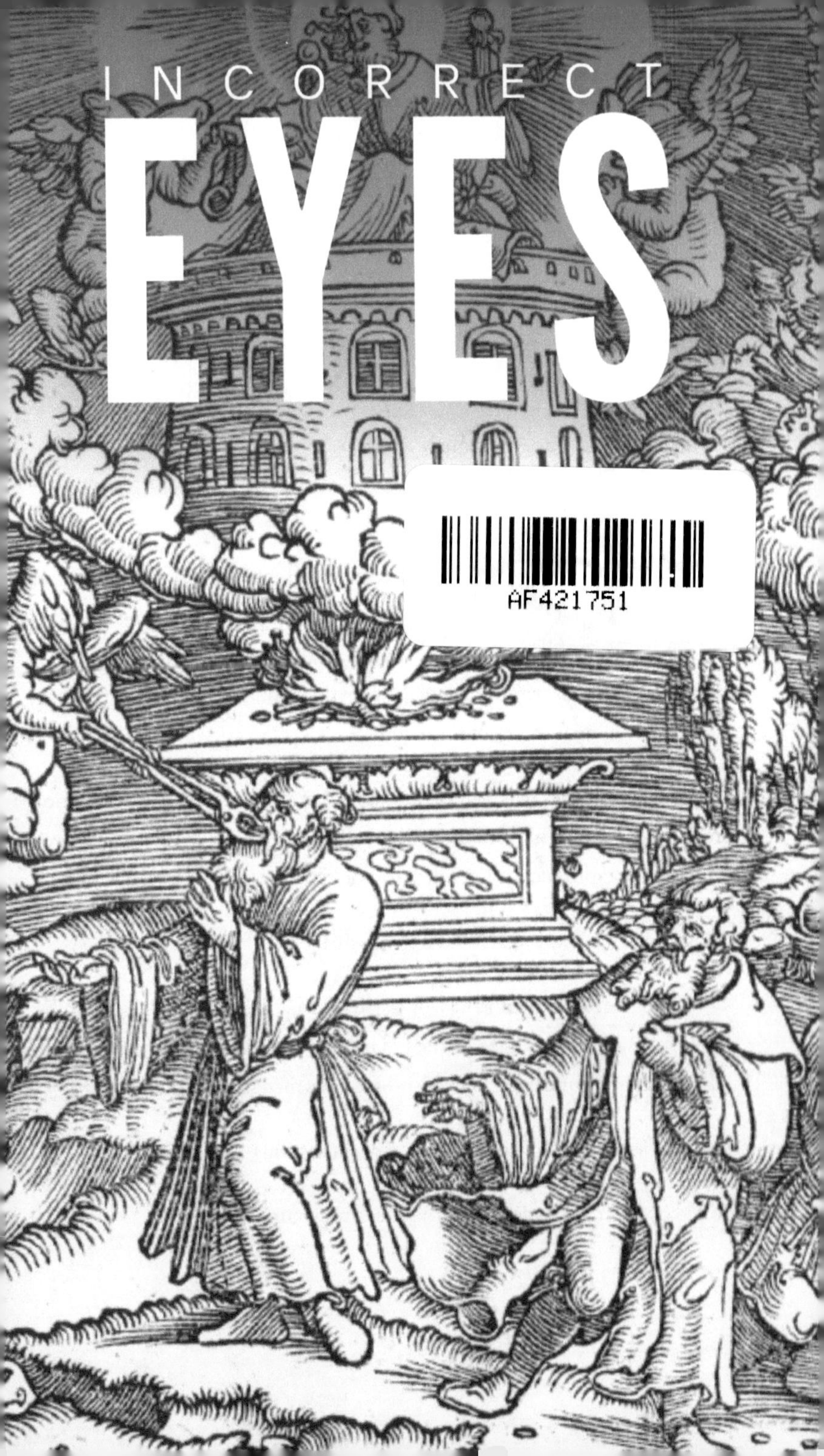

PRAISE FOR INCORRECT EYES

INCORRECT EYES is the definition of religious horror. Showing his range, Andromeda creates a story so vividly grotesque that you cannot stop reading. Equal parts unsettling and eldritch, Incorrect Eyes sets the nerves alight. It's a short story that will have your skin crawling days after. You cannot afford to skip this nightmare.

– Taylor Hubbard, author of *The Flowered Blade*

INCORRECT EYES is a fast-paced, eerie, and paranoia-inducing thrill-ride. Andromeda Ruins weaves dread into every bit of prose, and readers will spiral with the narrator into obsession and anxiety. This unique psychological spin on religious horror is a must-read.

– Tyler Battaglia, author of *Pray For Him*

INCORRECT EYES is a sweaty, feverish, unholy nightmare, not for the faint of heart. The quick pace and gorey prose will have you clenching your muscles. A perfect gut-churning bite-sized horror story.

– H.S. Wolfe, author of *ROTGUT*

Voicey and claustrophobic, ***INCORRECT EYES*** is a brisk read of paranoia and religious trauma in which Angels make their presence known to a student who took Be Not Afraid to heart. This narrative grabs the reader by the neck and holds their eyes wide open as the narrator grapples with divinity becoming distressingly real.

– Ladz, author of *The Fealty of Monsters*

INCORRECT EYES is a psychosis drenched must read that brings the reader through a thrilling yet unsettling religious experience. Andromeda Ruins has crafted a twisting narrative that leaves readers wanting more by the end. Highly recommend for a short, skin crawling read.

– Dorian Valentine, author of *Rosemary & Iron*

INCORRECT EYES is possibly the most interesting thing I've read this year. The prose is exquisite and the paranoia is incredibly well framed and well done. The religious element is well done too, and is disturbing without crossing any major lines. There is a fair number of disturbing incidents, but even those are incredibly well done. Even though the entire story really hit me under the ribcage it was still a great read and I would highly recommend it.

– Anita Primrose, author of the *Bonded Wings* series

A visceral story of obsession, exaltation, and isolation, **INCORRECT EYES** is a thrilling look into one person's descent into devotional madness. *RUINS* has crafted a gruesome, nauseating piece of thrilling horror that will stick with you, all consuming and soul devouring, for a long time.

ANDROMEDA RUINS

– Olive J. Kelley, author of *Junker Seven*

This book contains sensitive content. Be aware and read at your own risk.

Some topics include:

bodily mutilation, extreme paranoia, eye things (including disembodied eyes, being watched at all times, and removal of eyes), fear and terror, psychosis, possible misophonia and emetophobia, Catholicism (and the guilt associated with it), religious trauma, desecration of a church

IF YOUR RIGHT EYE CAUSES YOU TO SIN, TEAR IT OUT AND THROW IT AWAY. FOR IT IS BETTER THAT YOU LOSE ONE OF YOUR MEMBERS THAN THAT YOUR WHOLE BODY BE THROWN INTO HELL.

MATTHEW 5:28-29

BE NOT AFRAID.

My life changed when I heard those three words.

It wasn't an immediate change. No, it was a slow, crawling thing. I was raised a good Catholic kid, after all. Those three words were ones that I grew up with, ones that I am well acquainted with.

Sundays were always full of stories about the messengers of God, tales as great as They were that sung their praises. But, of course, any time the Angels were mentioned, the greeting wasn't far behind.

Be Not Afraid was a melody that hung in the background of my life over the soft harmonies of the church's organs, soothing me into complacency.

There was something about the messengers that never sat right with me, though. A sinking pit in my stomach when They were brought up, something deeply and unsettlingly *wrong*. I was too young to understand what that feeling was at the time, and when I tried to explain it to my mom she would say that I was a good God-fearing kid like I was supposed to be.

Then I left the church. We all knew it was coming, even if my mom acted surprised. I always asked too many questions, sought answers in anyone who would give me the light of day. The most common victim of my curiosity was the Father. He always did have endless patience. Until he didn't.

Maybe he didn't like grubby little kids who refused to play into the traditional gender roles his faith upheld. Maybe I, in particular, was annoying. Maybe I asked him one too many questions that bordered on heresy. All I know is that he was happy to see me go by the time I left town for college. It was an end to his own personal torment at the hands of a child.

So no, this wasn't an immediate change. It was a gradual descent into sleepless nights and haunting dreams. One I'm sure the Father would be delighted in if he were here. I should admonish myself for thinking so lowly of a man of Faith, but I know that man has been praying for my downfall in that ratty old country parish.

Maybe something answered his prayers. After so many years, maybe something finally moved to give the old man some vindications. I've spent so long studying the faith he so strictly believes in, after all, with the express intent of finding every little thing that doesn't make sense in it's scripture. Maybe that was enough for God to move on his behalf. Honestly, I should have seen it coming with the cynical eye I've had.

One thing I will give the Father, though, is that it is so very tempting to fall back into the Faith I was raised in when faced with the horror of what I've seen. The dreams—*no, nightmares*—I have been subjected to make no sense otherwise. The sheer terror I face every night when I go to sleep only to be greeted by a visage of Heavenly Light.

The nightmares don't make sense once removed from the context of Faith. How else do I explain seeing an Angel?

I don't. The Angels are a creation of humanity, something designed to add depth to our sacred texts. A fabrication to add intrigue to the words of Isaiah, Ezekiel, Revelation, and Enoch. They have to be creations, or else They wouldn't have been removed from the Christian canon. The Church may make questionable decisions, but they wouldn't erase the evidence of something as holy as an Angel, right?

And still there's a voice in my head that asks: *What if They weren't a fabrication? What if there truly are Angels out in the world?*

No. No, that isn't possible. What I saw in my dreams is simply an image given form due to stress. That's it!

I've just had my nose in the books for far too long, spent too many late nights reading the dense texts of the Tanakh. Yeah, I've just stretched myself too thin between my classes and my research. I just need to make it to the end of the semester so I can rest, then things will go back to normal.

'Normal' being shifting full focus onto my research, of course. I can't help dumping every waking second into it, this is what I've wanted to do my entire life. It came as a surprise, the email offering me this position. I almost missed it, then thought I was dreaming. Had to have my partner look at it and verify that it was real, that I was being asked to join a specialized team focused on researching the Messengers.

Needless to say, I quickly accepted the offer.

Why wouldn't I? It was a paid opportunity being handed to me, one that seemed to be specifically catered to my studies and personal interests. Truly, the offer was one of those 'too good to be true' moments. Only it never fell out from under me.

I was pleasantly surprised when I met the team, quickly becoming integrated in the atmosphere. The group is unique, but that's normal for this area of study. Getting to know everyone was decently easy: after spending days, weeks, months reading dense and heavy ancient prose, one develops a need to talk and talk and talk when given the option. I took advantage of that, asking each person about their interests and why they joined the team.

Most of the team had the same answers I did: this is a fully funded research team with access to the rare and ancient texts housed at one of the oldest colleges in the country. We would have been fools to pass this up.

And so we spend our days scanning each and every word on the crumbling parchment and papyri, analyzing digital scans of scrolls we can't even open, trying to see into the past through their words. Trying to figure out why the texts about the Angels changed. Trying to prove that the Angels are fantastical creations like I so desperately pray that They are.

All day every day is spent searching for the one missing piece of the puzzle, the one small detail that will make everything else fall into place. Once that happens, and I graduate, I'll finally be able to move on with my life.

Yet, we've found nothing. In over a year of our search, we've come up empty handed. Not one stray piece of information, nothing. The only thing we've—*that I've, God I hope this is only happening to me*—gained from our search is a severe caffeine addiction fueled by rampant paranoia.

Paranoia... paranoia... that word makes me sound insane. Me? Paranoid? Over a dream?

Yeah. I am. I am paranoid. I feel as if I'm being watched at all hours of the day and it's overwhelming.

I don't know what to do anymore. I'm being watched when I'm awake and being confronted with stress dreams when I'm asleep. I tried talking to my therapist about the dreams, about my lack of sleep, but she says that it's nothing to worry about, that I am going through one of God's tests. I don't know how to tell her that if this is a test sent by God then I don't want to believe anymore.

Even when I sleep I get no rest, relying on energy drinks to survive. The caffeine addiction comes with trade-offs, but I can't convince myself to care. They make me jittery and nauseous at all hours of the day. I can avoid the creations of my mind that haunt my nightmares, but I've started making mistakes. I've become sloppy in my work. My notes are gibberish and my teammates have started to notice.

Their concerned questions started off innocent enough:

"Hey, how are you doing?" spoken softly, as if they are afraid of scaring me off.

"Did you get any sleep last night?" asked during lunch as they watch me crack open another neon can.

I know they mean well, but their concern is bearing down on my soul in a way I cannot handle. It pains me to know that I am causing so much grief. I was never meant to be the focus of their attention. But now that I am, something's changed. Maybe it's always been this way and I was never in a position to notice, but I can't look them in the eyes anymore.

I don't know why, I can't explain it. There is just something in their gaze that feels wrong. *Something is wrong.*

The guilt eats away at me until I shift my schedule. Small excuses start to pile up, little white lies meant to make the transition easier.

"Oh, I've started sleeping in" and "I picked up a morning class this semester" fall out of my mouth when they ask why I'm coming in later and later every day. It took about a month, but now I'm coming into the library hours after everyone's gone home.

The graveyard shift suits me better anyways. Fewer people around to see my slow spiral into whatever this is. Just me and the sinking feeling of being watched while I stick my nose into ancient texts and search for an answer that's different than the one I suspect to be true in my gut:

The Angels are real, and They are watching.

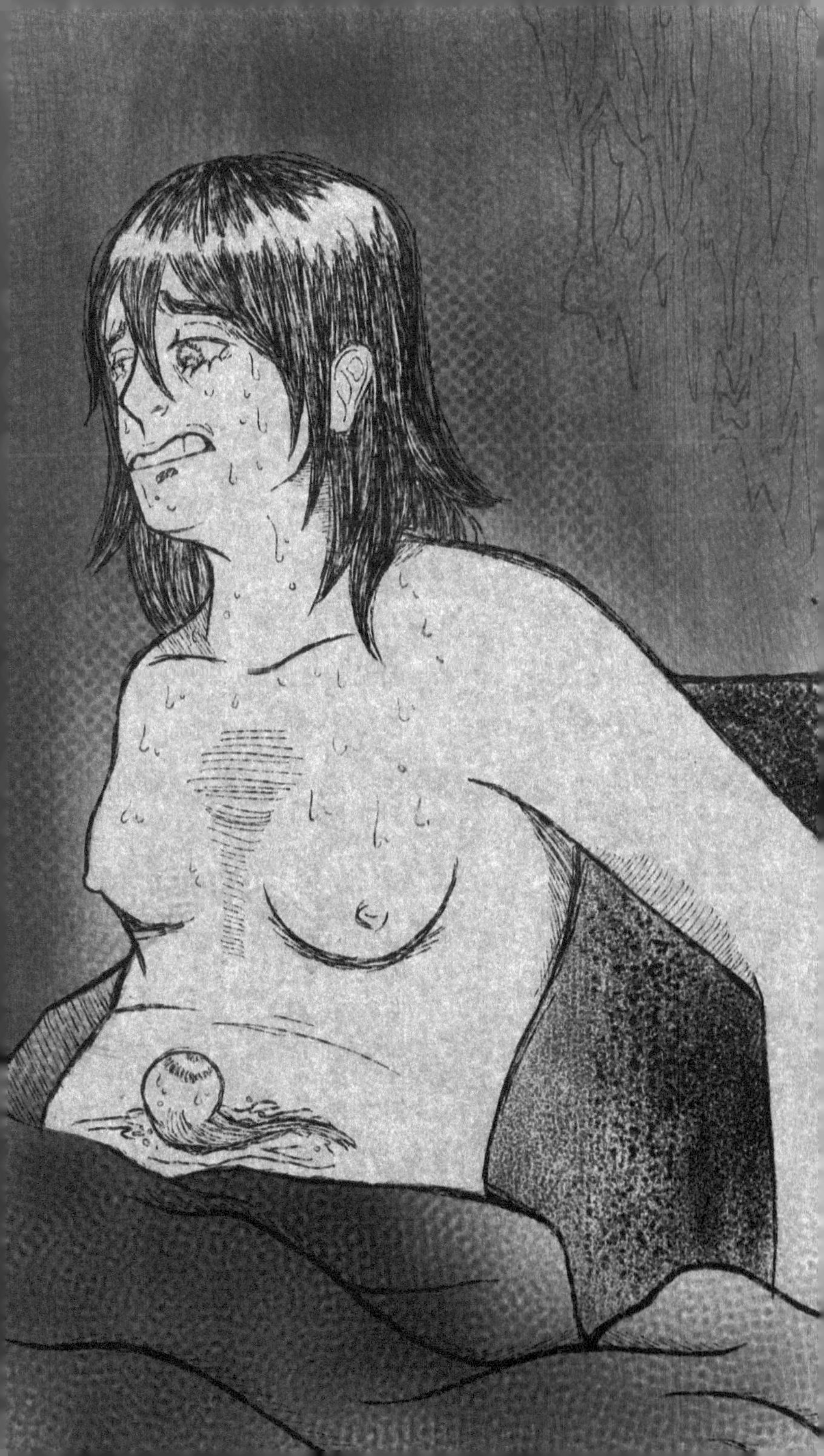

I CAN SEE THEM *everywhere*.

Or, rather, I can see their Eyes. The free-floating sentinels They use to watch my every move.

When They started following me about a month ago, I came to realize that the Angels are real—despite not yet having proof—and the next morning I woke up to something cold and wet on my chest. A slimy Eye, one only I could see. I'll never forget how my partner looked at me in fear after I woke them to my screaming. It was the first time they'd been afraid of me, and I pray I'll never see that look in their eyes again.

Now the Eyes stalk me, follow me every hour of the day. Hover in the dark. Decorate the corners of my vision and remind me that I am never alone.

There's still a part of my brain that refuses to believe the Eyes are real. I mean, I can see Them hovering around me, but a small voice of reason in my head tells me that They could just be hallucinations. Before I stopped going to therapy, my therapist told me about stress hallucinations. She said it was possible for the brain to get so overloaded that it starts to perceive things shifting in the peripheries. Eventually, she said, those small shifts could take on a more familiar shape.

For me, that's the one thing I have a hard time looking at: Eyes.

It's not that hard to imagine myself becoming a victim of stress hallucinations. Finals have been Hell, especially now that I'm barely sleeping. My entire degree is on the line if I don't pass my classes, but I can't bring myself to care all that much when my sanity is at risk. If that isn't bad enough, I also haven't been able to eat. I am willing to bet that I have energy drinks running through my veins instead of blood, which doesn't help. Nausea has become my best friend.

Everything put together paints the picture of a dying man, and I wouldn't be surprised if I started hallucinating because of it.

Either way, it's better than the alternative. I'd very much like to push the reality of what I'm seeing to the back of my mind, to listen to the small voice telling me that I'm just tired.

God, is it bad that I'd rather lose my mind like this than have tangible proof that the Angels are real?

Hell, maybe I can blame the incessant buzzing of my phone as the final push over the edge into madness. I had it on silent for a while, but the silence is more disturbing. It leaves room for doubt, room for my brain to convince me that none of this is real.

No, the buzzing of my phone, while annoying, keeps me sane. Now the back-track of my life has become the sound of vibrating on a wooden desk as my screen lights up with messages from teammates, friends, *family* that I just can't bring myself to answer. I don't... I don't know how to answer them.

> **Are you okay?**

How does one define 'okay'? Physically, I'm alive. Mentally? I don't know how to answer that. I haven't been able to feel anything other than fear and nausea for months.

> Where have you been?

Hiding. Hiding and working and sinking further and further into the pits of despair and paranoia.

> Your friends are wondering where you are. They're worried about you.

I wonder where I am, too. Where am I? What am I doing? What are these words I surround myself with? And what do they mean? *Why are there Eyes everywhere?*

I don't know what to do anymore, I'm afraid I've lost my mind. I can't sleep, can't breathe, can't even think without being observed. I desperately need to escape and I don't know how to.

The wooden desk rattles as I slam my hands down. *God*, I am so sick of this shit! I just want to sleep again, I want to go home and sleep with my partner. I want to be normal again, free from the terrors that plague my every waking moment.

But I'm here instead. Heaving as I stand over crumpled papers and smudged writing, with tears and sweat dripping down my face.

My breath rattles as I try to calm myself. Panicking now will do me no favors, especially not when I am alone. I need to calm down and return to my search. I can't risk accidentally damaging the texts laid out on the table.

Emotions clog my throat as I close my eyes. It's hard to breathe still, a painful pressure constricting my chest. I focus on my breathing. In around the surge of emotion, further down into my lungs with a tickling sensation, hold for a half a second before I'm forced to exhale with a disquieting wheeze.

I've made it this far, I can make it through just one. More. Night.

It's not long before the squelching sounds of slimy Eyes start to encroach on me, glitching feathers floating in front of my eyes. I take one more strangled breath in before snapping my eyes open and pushing myself towards my coat hanging on the door. My hands frantically dip into all the pockets, searching for the little red inhaler I carry on my person.

Finding nothing, I return to my seat. *Fuck*, I hope it's in my backpack. I'll never hear the end of it if I have to go to the Emergency Room because I forgot the stupid piece of plastic at home again.

In a stroke of luck, I find my inhaler in the front pouch full of pens. The medicine does it's job, loosening up my lung as I take in a puff with a bone-shaking cough. The second goes down much easier.

Once I'm certain I can breathe again, I turn back to the table. The papers are scattered, disorganized and strewn about from my outburst. Some of them are creased, all of them covered in the chicken scratch that my writing has become these days.

I don't know where to start in attempting to understand the notes, the shear amount of illegible information in front of me is overwhelming. So I don't, opting to pile the papers and set them aside.

Time to start fresh. Just a clean sheet of paper, a pencil, and Isaiah.

It's a passage I've read time and time again. One I could likely recite by heart, if I really tried. One that's haunted me my entire life for reasons I refuse to acknowledge. I haven't found anything in the words yet, but I can't shake the feeling that the answers my team has been searching for are here.

In the year that King Uzziah died, I saw the
Lord seated on a high and lofty throne, and His
robe[lit. seam] filled the temple.

Pretty standard religious imagery, if I do say so myself. To
see the Lord our God sitting on a high and lofty throne.
There's an asterisk next to the word robe, though, and when
I look at the notes in my translation guide I find out why.
Apparently there is a discrepancy with the word that this
text—and many others—translate as robe. The professor
that wrote this translation notes that it could mean 'seam'
or 'train'.

That's not my focus, but it could be. Small discrepancies in
translations are where I'm going to find my answers, I can
feel it.

Seraphim[lit. Heavenly beings] were standing
above Him;

Them. There's another asterisk, another note about a discrepancy. This time in relation to the Seraphim Themselves,
that the word would be broken down to mean Heavenly

Beings. But we all know what they are. Angels, Messengers, Seraphim... they all mean the same Creature.

Just reading the name causes my breath to catch. Tension thickens the air. I know what comes next, an image straight from my nightmares:

> each one had six wings: with two he covered his face, with two he covered his feet, and with two he flew.

Exactly how they appeared in my dreams. Only, this description has a distinct lack of Eyes. Not for a lack of trying on my part. Messy sketches of eyes decorate the margins of the replica, scattered around the words describing the Holy Being.

Surely, there has to be a mention of the Eyes. There has to be, somewhere in the texts. Maybe in a fragment? I'll have to cross reference them in a moment.

For now, I can feel my soul being drawn to the next section of the text. There is a burning needs in my gut to continue.

Holy, holy, holy is the Lord of Hosts;
His glory fills the whole earth.

I can remember what the Father told me to believe in church all those years ago. Remember how he guided me in prayer after I asked about this description and why is was so scary. He told me that the chants of the Angels were something to be heard, that They could lift a soul and bring it closer to God.

But when I read the words on the page I return to the question the small child I used to be asked. Why is it so scary? I can't hear their chants, my ears are filled with Their screaming and wailing. Their shouts beg for atonement and forgiveness.

Images pop unbidden into my mind: Angels as we knew them growing up, human-like and innocent. But now They have tears of viscous blood streaming down Their faces as They grovel before His throne, screaming and begging for His warmth. Seraphim and Cherubim just behind Them, blocking the pathetic Angels in, forcing Them to submit to His holy gaze.

Their screams harmonize in the worst ways, ringing through my mind and spilling through my ears. The mind-numbing pain They cause is only worsened as my eyes are drawn further down the page.

> Woe is me for I am ruined [must be silent]
> because I am a man of unclean lips
> and live among a people of unclean lips,
> and because my eyes have seen the King,
> the Lord of Hosts.

Unclean, unclean, *unclean*. The word repeats in my mind, tearing through the chorus of terror put forward by the Angels. I am unclean, just like he was. I live among people with unclean Eyes, just as he with lips. He—I—*we* are RUINED.

My mind conjured the image of the next paragraph. Of the Seraphim flying towards me—Isaiah—*us* holding a glowing coal by means of a pair of tongs. From the altar is comes. As it lays the burning stone in my eyes, it speaks:

Now that this has touched your lips,
your wickedness is removed
and your sin is atoned for.

Then I scream.

Pencils and pens clatter to the floor, papers floating through the air behind them as I throw everything out of my sight. My voice tapers off—am I screaming? Is that me?—as I come back to the cramped study room. I need fresh air. I can't stand one more moment in here. The sterile white walls are closing in on me, suffocating me with their cold paint-covered bricks. Maybe I'll take a quick break, step out for a moment to gather myself.

I lean forward, pressing my elbows into the rough grain wood of the desk and cradling my forehead in my hands. I'm so fucking exhausted. I'm so tired of the constant anxiety and all-consuming paranoia. Tears sting the backs of my eyes as I try to hold them in. I don't want to cry, I just want everything to be done. I want to relax.

But I can't. Each breath I take in—*a natural process that every person can do properly, except for me*—makes things worse. They hit shallower and shallower until I'm barely breathing in at all. Hyperventilating would be a better word for it.

The rough feeling of my hands scraping down my face soothes me in a weird way, allowing me to take in one normal breath, then, after a moment, another. The small amount of control I've gained gives me the confidence to look back down at the desk. A mistake.

My vision doubles as I try to focus on the papyri replicas of the Septuagint and Masoretic texts, fragments sprinkled on top like ancient confetti. My hands clench where they rest on my face, fingernails digging into the soft flesh of my cheeks and undoubtedly drawing blood.

Frustration builds as the texts swim in my vision. It's already taking so much out of me to study just one copy of each text, let alone having to compare it to so many fragments and second-hand accounts. And to make it worse, I can't seem to figure out where the fragments go, can't figure out where they fit into the narrative or what they're talking about or why they were removed from the longer canon scriptures. The longer I look, the more the words distort, separating themselves from the scans of papyri, twisting and turning around one another to form incomprehensible strings of Greco-Latinate letters.

My breath catches in my throat as those strings start to form crude Eyes, blinking at me as they mock my inability to focus.

Fuck, I need a break.

I push myself up and away from the desk, scrambling away from the threatening Eyes. My back hits the cold brick of the study room far too soon, not giving me nearly enough space. Not getting me far enough away.

The smooth paint covering the bricks does little to stop the corners from digging into my back as I slide down until I'm squatting and pushing my weight back into the wall, my hands splayed out on the bricks beside me. Movement is normally enough to make whatever I'm seeing disappear, but the Eyes are *still there*. They are still hovering above the desk, staring down at me in disdain.

I can't control my breathing anymore, the small thread of control I won back has been severed as the air gets stuck in my lungs. It burns, holding my breath like this. But I don't care as the Eyes start to drift closer to me. I need to look away, I need to blink, I need to do *something* to make Them go away but I can't. I can't and They're getting closer and I need to leave but I Can't. Look. Away.

The room starts heating up, the previously cold brick behind me is scalding the bare skin of my arms where my tank top doesn't cover. The room is cooking me alive and the Eyes are still *getting closer*. The shadows in the corners of my vision start creeping forward, tendrils darting out to meet the Eyes of text as I helplessly watch. It's a battle over what will happen first, will the shadows swallow my vision or will the Eyes reach me?

I get my answer when my vision fades and I collapse onto the ground. My knees hit the linoleum floor hard, a sickening crack resonates in my mind as I'm finally able to take a breath in. My throat burns, my lungs constrict. The air I'm able to take in is limited, but it's still something.

Moving is painful as I shift myself into sitting on the floor, crossing my legs and pressing my back against the wall that is cool once again. My vision starts to return, small spots of light appearing amongst the mass of black. I tilt my head back until it thunks against the wall. Everything is blurry, but at least everything's back to normal. There are no Eyes, no tendrils of darkness in the corners. I'm alone again. *Thank God.*

I sit there for a moment as my senses come back to me in full. Breathing is still hard, and as I stand up I grab my inhaler off the desk. The small plastic device hasn't gotten this much use in years, not since I was told that I 'outgrew' my asthma when I was in middle school. What a lie that was, even all these years later I still can't function like a normal person.

It's time to get out of this room, I need to get some fresh air. The texts lay where I left them on the desk and I don't bother to clean them up, barely sparing a glance at them in fear of what I'll see. It's not like I'll be gone long, anyways.

The door clicks shut behind me as I step into the main room of the library and pat down my pockets. I have my lanyard and nothing else. *Fuck.* The door thankfully hasn't locked yet when I turn around and re-enter the study room to grab my phone off the desk.

My coat is still hanging on the door and I consider grabbing it, but I don't plan on being outside long enough to warrant it. I do, however, reach into the pocket for my switchblade before grabbing the hoodie that rests on the hook below it. The last thing I need right now is to go outside for a quick break and end up getting mugged, a concern I never had until I started working in the dead of night. Maybe I'm being paranoid again, but I know my luck and honestly I wouldn't be surprised if it happened.

I chance a look at the clock on the wall as I slip the oversized hoodie over my shoulders, the zipper snagging halfway up as it always has, but I pay that no mind as I try to see how long I can reasonably spend on a break. Looks like the damned thing is broken, though. It shows 1:07 AM, but that's not possible. There's no way in Hell that I've already been here for five hours.

But when I look at my phone to double check, it says the same thing. 1:07 AM. I watch as it switches to 1:08 AM. I really have been in here for five hours already, holy shit.

Hopefully this means that the rest of the night will go by just as fast, though I could do without the... whatever it was that happened. I just want to go home. My love would know what to do, how to deal with whatever sick game my mind is playing on me.

The door clicks shut behind me, and this time I don't go back.

The harsh yellow fluorescence pouring through the window of the study room is the only source of light as I make my way through the shelves of books in the main hall. I keep my head down as I walk, trying to push through the unease that has accompanied me for the past three weeks.

There are Eyes out here, too, though I pretend not to notice them. These ones aren't made out of words. They look real. Disembodied Eyes, plucked straight out of... I don't want to know. They taunt and jeer at me from where They're tucked between the ancient volumes on the shelves. I don't look up at Them, keeping my eyes glued to the worn gray carpet below my feet as I repeat "just keep walking" to myself.

What was once a place of comfort has become anything but.

My gaze darts back and forth as the Eyes begin to move in my peripheries. They roll out of Their crevices, leaving wet trails in Their path. I nervously swallow as I listen to the sounds of the Eyes moving, squelching obscenely as They bump into one another and squeeze between the books. The sound makes my stomach turn.

The air grows thick as my lungs constrict. My hand clenches in the thin fabric of my ratty tank top just above my heart as I try to get my lungs to work as they should. The sounds are too much, the Eyes are too much. I pretend not to notice as the hairs on the back of my neck raise. Pretend not to notice as the eyes stop moving, wet noises falling silent as They turn to look behind me. Pretend not to notice when I feel *something* fill the space of the aisle.

My shadow grows on the ground before me, stretching as it tries to escape before I do. The air is heavy, thick in my lungs, and I can no longer pretend that I have control over my breathing.

I need out. How long is this aisle? I need to leave. How long have I been walking? Why haven't I reached the door? Why are the walls *getting closer?*

My steps falter, but I refuse to stop moving. Two long strides make up the distance my stumble cost me. The walls are getting closer, bringing the Eyes closer to me, aren't They? No. No, that's not possible. Library shelves don't move on their own and they don't house actual eyes. I'm just imagining this. They have to be hallucinations. Figments of my imagination, manifestations of the stress I'm experiencing. Right?

My hand tremble and I quickly untangle them from my tank top and shove them into the pockets of my hoodie to hide the sign of my weakness. Weakness in the face of squelching, of swarming in the dark, of the warmth at my back, of the terror deep in my bones.

I need out. I need out, out, *out, out,* **OUT.**

THE DOORS SLAM OPEN as I hurtle my body weight through them. The impact slows me for only a moment before I'm stumbling through the threshold and falling down the steps in front of the building. I land hard on my knees and wrists, sliding across the concrete until I finally come to a stop. Streaks of red decorate the rough concrete, they're all I'm able to focus on as I try to rein in my ragged breathing.

My heart pounds, my blood rushes in my ears. The swarm of Eyes that had been following disperses into the corners of my vision once again, leaving me alone as I writhe in pain on the cold hard sidewalk.

I hate this. I fucking hate all of this. I'm being used for entertainment, thrown around like a toy for something greater to watch. It makes me feel small, useless. Makes me want to crumple in on myself until there is nothing left.

Water droplets stain the concrete below me as I cry. My head bows until my forehead kisses the ground and I let it all out. I try not to scream, I really do. Instead, I hear the pathetic whimpers that fall from my mouth as I let the pain run through my body.

As I roll onto my back, the wounds on my hands and knees start to sting. The cold December air caresses the gore as rivulets of blood drip down my skin. My arms are splayed out, the palms of my hands face the heavens above as I try and collect myself. A faint wheeze accompanies each breath I take, thankfully growing fainter the more air I take in. The chill of the night seeps into my bones.

The stars are visible tonight, twinkling lights litter the cloudless night sky. An odd sight this far into the city, what with the city's light pollution and all. I thought it would be impossible to see the celestial bodies.

As impossible as it sounds, the twinkling lights hundreds of millions of light years away make me feel less alone.

I wish I could talk to them, wish I could spill my guts to the balls of gas that illuminate the sky every night. They would listen. They would understand.

I reach for them, reach for the beings that could take me away from this pain, away from this insanity. *God,* I wish I could be with them.

Maybe one day I will join them, leave my mortal vessel behind and travel the heavens. Spend the eons learning anything and everything I can from the immortal skies. Maybe one day...

The stars disappear from my vision as I close my eyes for a moment, taking time to breathe and exist where I am. My arm falls back down to the rough concrete as I take a deep breath in. I know the stars are still there, but for a moment I imagine them fading away, leaving me alone once again on the cold hard ground.

The vibration of footsteps around me tells me that I need to stand up. That I need to get out of people's way. Surely I made a scene with my hasty exit from the library, that's undoubtedly what the din of voices around me are talking about as they murmur amongst themselves.

The stars are still there when I open my eyes, like I knew they would be. They hang in the black abyss of night, keeping watch over me as I struggle to sit up. I try to aid myself by pushing against the concrete, only to be rudely reminded of the open wounds on the heels of my hands. It's a struggle, but I manage to sit up and lean forward, wincing as I pull my hands in front of me and rest the backs on my gore-wrought knees to assess the damage.

Bloody and raw. Great. There are black spots of debris mixed in with the oozing gunk that once was the heel of my palm. I need to find a first aid kit and some anti-septic as soon as I can. The chance that a random person on the street has what I need is slim, but it wouldn't hurt to ask, right?

When I look up I find that everyone is giving me a wide berth. Actually, that might not be a strong enough way to describe their actions. Everyone is either on the sidewalk across the street or walking in the street on their way over there, making sure to stay as far away from me as they physically can. I watch as a group of people—a family—walk further down the street, only to cross back over to this side of the road. Most likely as soon as they deem themselves far enough away from the pathetic man having an episode in front of the library.

Now that I think about it, why are there so many people out and avoiding me? It's the middle of the night. I can understand a straggler here or there given that we're in the city, but this many people? This isn't normal.

Standing up is a Sisyphean task, I have to lean to the side and swing my weight around until I can stumble to get my feet under me without leaning forward onto my knees. Then I have to be careful about how I steady myself, using a painfully closed fist instead of pressing my open wounds to the concrete. The movement is unsteady, but I'd rather not make things any worse for myself than they already are. Especially knowing that I'll have to wrap my hands well enough to avoid getting blood on my notes when I return.

I stretch my arms out in the cold night air as I try to catch my balance, my elbows clicking in retaliation. *Breathe in, two, three. Breathe out, two, three.* I haven't fallen yet, so I should be fine. It's tempting to brush the dirt and debris from my clothes but I know I shouldn't, that it would just risk getting into the already dirty gore on my hands. No, I will have to wait until my wounds are dealt with.

The itch to check my phone is strong, but the same precautions apply there. I shouldn't reach my hand into my pocket until I take care of my hands, especially not into a tight jean pocket. That's just asking for blood to be smeared everywhere and an infection to set in. I huff and close my eyes, mentally fighting myself for being so reckless. Over what? A creation of my own overactive imagination?

I'm better than this, I should be able to hold myself together better and avoid acting so irresponsibly. Especially when I'm on the clock.

Schooling my thoughts, I open my eyes and search for any way to figure out what time it is. I should just head back inside, but I haven't convinced myself yet. I can convince my brain that everything has been the result of my lack of sleep and imagination, but there is a primal part of me that says I shouldn't return to where that *thing* was. That it's a predator and I am it's prey.

Every person I try and approach on the street looks at me in fear before rushing away, herding their children, in clothes nicer than I've ever owned, away from me. That's fair, I suppose.

It takes me walking two blocks down to find someone, anyone, who will tell me the time and I don't believe them. It can't be 3 AM, I refuse to believe it. I left the study room a little after 1 AM, there's no way that I spent two fucking hours navigating the aisle of books.

But when they show me the screen of their phone, that's exactly what it says. 3:05 AM.

More importantly, though, is the date shown just below the large numbers. Sunday, December 25th. Christmas.

Fuck, I missed midnight mass.

I was supposed to go with my mom, she's probably worried sick. My hand twitches at my side, itching to dig into my pocket and check my notifications. I will have to call her when I get my hands situated, explain to her why I missed mass on tonight of all nights after promising her I would be there. She'll understand. I hope.

Then again, she'll probably just tell me what my therapist told me before I stopped going.

I shove the thought of my mother to the back of my mind as I thank the stranger and continue walking down the block. At least it makes sense why there are so many people out now. The library is close to a university campus, and therefore is close to about five different churches of various denominations. The people milling about around me are likely headed home after a long night of praying for salvation at the hands of an infant.

The uneasy feeling of being watched resurfaces with each step I take away from the library. While the crowd was pretty sparse at first, the streets are now bursting with idle bodies. I keep my head down as I walk, trying to blend in and avoid the nigh unavoidable amount of people who are suddenly around me. After bumping into a third person, I look up. I don't stop moving, but my gaze scans the crowd to try and find any gaps in which I can escape the throng of people.

The longer I look, the more people there are. It's as if they are manifesting in front of my very eyes, filling in any and every empty space, and sucking the fresh air out of my lungs.

My stride slows as my nerves take over, attempting to freeze me in place. My eyes dart from person to person as I stop dead in my tracks. Watching. Observing. Trying to keep attention off of myself and making myself as invisible as I can while standing in the middle of a large crowd that has not stopped moving around me. I ebb and sway with the flow, the push and pull reminding me of when my mom would take me swimming in the lake near our home.

Only now I'm on my own, and I'm terrified.

Crowds have never been my favorite thing in the world, I've always been more of an independent studies person. But tonight has been pushing my limits on all fronts, and this is no different. The waves of people crash into me, constricting the space around me and forcing me to move with them, or drown where I am.

Someone pushes me to the right and a ripple flows through the crowd, showing small gaps between the people—*the Eyes are hiding in those spaces*—for the briefest of moments before the ripple makes it's way back to me.

The longer I am held there the more I see: Eyes dancing and weaving through the over-packed crowd, any and every blank space filled with Their pulsing and oozing. I can hear Them being squished between swaying bodies, squelching as They burst, spraying Their holy viscera on the bystanders.

How do they not see Them? How do they not hear Them?

I'm not sure what's emboldened the Eyes, what's empowered Them to venture out of the recesses of my paranoid mind and into the crowds of Main Street, but the fact that no one else is reacting to Them simultaneously terrifies me and puts me at ease. That tells me that They are in my head, and only my head. But They aren't just in my head, it's like They've evolved and found a new habitat to thrive in. Like They're forcing me to face Their disembodied form head-on.

I'm losing my fucking mind.

A hand lands heavy on my shoulder, startling me and causing the crowd to disappear into thin air. Just like that, the surge of people fades into the slightly above tolerable amount that I remember being on the street when I asked that stranger for the time.

There's a voice behind me, asking me something, *something*, but I can't make out what. I can hear them just fine, but the words blend and mix in my mind like soup. I turn to face them, to try and be polite and deal with the consequences of a clear spiral in mental health, but when I look up there's something wrong. Their eyes are wrong, they're *wrong*.

Those are not human eyes.

I don't know what they are, but I know they are not human. I scramble to categorize them, to find a logical explanation for why they're not right but I can't... I don't know what they are.

Incorrect. They are incorrect.

Those *things* squint as they flinch away from me. My own scream seems distant to my ears, but I take the opening it's given me and I run. I can feel the eyes—*incorrect, they're incorrect; what are they?*—of more bystanders on me as I do. I need to get away, I need to hide. Why are they watching me?

I keep my head ducked as I run, trying to get as far away as possible. I don't know where I'm headed, just that I need to *get away.*

I SEE THE RAISED edge of the cracked sidewalk before my foot catches on it, but it's too late to catch myself. As I fall, I realize I don't have time to turn, landing hard on my already torn up knees and hands with a yelp.

Blood pools under my hands, the wounds that had finally started to scab over are torn open once again. I can see a faint reflection in the blood, something that looks almost like a wing. But when I look back over my shoulder there's nothing, just an empty street. I swing my gaze around to see where I am, only to be greeted with a silent city.

I push myself back, balancing in a squat on my heels as I try and figure out where I'm at now. The buildings around here are all very nondescript. Well, except for the Catholic Church across the street. It's a beautiful building, gorgeous

Gothic architecture with stunning arches and awe-inspiring stained glass windows. But it doesn't feel right. Something nags at me, tells me that I shouldn't be in front of a church so late.

Maybe it's the gargoyles, large and imposing on the buttresses of the building. They feel rather out of place this far into the city.

I divert my eyes, swallowing the lump of guilt that has pooled in my throat. *How am I going to explain this to my mom? Will I ever forgive myself for missing our plans?* It looks like there is a convenience store at the end of the block, the neon lights beckon me towards it. My steps are unsteady as I head across the street. The blood from my wounds runs rivers down my hands and my legs. I really need to staunch and wrap them.

But when I get to the end of the block, I realize the store is devoid of life. The doors are unlocked, but all of the lights are off and no one is in the back room when I check.

Odd.

I could just take the gauze that's sitting on the shelf, but I've already disappointed my mom so much tonight. My conscious cannot handle having to add stealing to that list.

No. I'll just have to find somewhere else to get gauze. For the time being I use the sleeve of my hoodie to wipe away the blood. It works well enough, I suppose. I'll have to remember to ask my partner to wash it if I make it home. If? No, no. *When* I get home. That's what I meant.

Stepping back out into the frigid winter air sends a chill down my spine. It feels much colder than it did when I entered the store. It's not common for temperatures to shift so much, but not necessarily unheard of in this area, even if it feels like it's tied to everything that's gone wrong so far tonight.

My hands are shaking, adrenaline finally wearing off, as I turn left and walk back towards the library. At this rate, I should just go back and see what first aid the building has. It'll probably be time for the morning shift librarian to come in by the time I return. She'll be able to help me.

But as I pass the church again, I stop. The church is beautiful; stark in contrast to the buildings around it. It puts them to shame, just as I remember my pastor back home doing. Shame. The one thing the church accurately teaches. Well, that and guilt. Two sides of the same coin, both telling me that I fucked up. What did I do? Doesn't matter, I'm going to Hell either way.

There's a glint of something in the stained glass windows—*almost like eyes tilted down on me in condescension*—that asks me to come inside. Asks me to enter the confessional, to pray for my soul despite the years of sin I've accumulated since I've left the church. Despite the fact that I've turned my back on God. Despite everything.

The voice of logic that told me to keep walking earlier returns, telling me to keep making my way back to the library. It tells me that I am unsafe in the House of the Lord.

But my curiosity wins out and I step up to the large wooden doors. A paper plastered onto the wood tells me that the church is closed until 2 PM today. Of course it is, it's the middle of the night hours, way past midnight mass at this point. The pastor has undoubtedly left and locked the doors. I raise my hand to trace the intricate carvings in the wood, running my fingers over the peaks and valleys as disappointment crawls up my throat.

I'm just about to acquiesce to the pit of dread forming in my stomach when the door creaks open. I shouldn't go in there, but I want to so bad and I don't know why. I haven't stepped foot on consecrated ground since the day my pastor told me to get out. I should heed the warning my instincts are giving me and return to the library.

But it's a church, right? What harm could it do?

I could go in there, slide into a pew, and pray like my therapist told me to do the last time I was in her office. She always did try to get me to go back, tried telling me that everything going wrong in my life was because I left the church. That I needed to repent and return to His arms.

Maybe she's right.

I push the door further open and walk through the threshold of the church, ignoring overwhelming sense of dread that tells me I'm making a mistake.

The church is even more beautiful on the inside. The silver moonlight filters through the stained glass windows, catching on the dust in the air and lighting up the nave in a way that I've only ever seen in religious art. It is a sight that people the like of me are never meant to see, and it brings a small smile to my face. Peace washes over me, tells me that I made a good decision when I entered the building. I can feel the tension bleeding from my joints, my body relaxing for the first time in months.

I would love to walk further into the church, to sit in a pew and pray for salvation, but I can't. I'm rooted to the spot, my peace becoming overwhelmed with thoughts I cannot control. Ones that tell me that I don't belong here. I haven't in a long, long time.

I turn to leave, my hand pressed up against the smooth interior of the closed door. When had the door closed? I know I didn't shut it behind me. Before I can pull the door open I feel a presence behind me. My shadow is creeping up the wood of the door, growing taller and taller in front of me despite my lack of movement.

The chill of the night is gone in an instant, replaced with a crackling heat and thick tension. The light around my shadow grows brighter, burning the wood and sending tendrils of smoke into the air.

The presence begs me to turn around, to face it.

I don't want to.

I ignored the fear in my stomach earlier, but not this time. I don't know what's behind me, and I don't want to know. I would rather burn to death in ignorance.

Maybe if I ignore it for long enough, if I tolerate the burning heat for long enough, it will go away. Maybe it will leave me alone.

It doesn't.

The hair on the back of my neck rises as a voice—*or what I can only describe as a voice; it's more like an amalgamation, a constant harmony of screeches*—reverberates through my bones. The stench of burning hair reaches my nose not long after.

BE NOT AFRAID.

No. Not this again. Not those words. Not here.

I'm fighting my own body, struggling to stay where I am instead of turning. Every fiber of my being demands that I give in, that I listen to the vibrations and turn around. But I don't want to. Guilt claws at my heart, tells me to supplicate myself before the Being so clearly Holy, like the good little Catholic boy I was raised. But I'm not that kid anymore and I have nothing to offer the Angel.

BE NOT AFRAID. FACE US.

I cannot resist any longer. I can feel my free will being stripped from my soul. My limbs go slack, arms falling uselessly to my side as I am forced to observe my body turning to face the Angel.

At first, the heavenly light blinds me. Nothing is visible as my eyes burn. I would scream if I could, but as it stands, the pain has no outlet. I am forced to stand there as the light burns, and it hurts, *it hurts,* **it hurts.**

Slowly, ever so slowly, my vision returns to me. I become accustomed to the burning and blinding light, but what is revealed isn't any better. My mind melts as my eyes devour the sight in front of me.

It looks exactly as Isaiah described, exactly as I saw in my nightmares.

Six wings.

Two—the purest of white with golden dipped feathers—overlap and cover what I must assume is the Angel's face. Most of it, at least. It's jaw is visible just underneath. Clean and pristine, until it isn't. A glitching overlay appears sporadically, as if there are two forms trying to take form at the same place. Trying to sustain the Angel in a realm it doesn't belong, before my very eyes.

In one the Angel is perfect. Holy in the ways we were taught growing up. In the other, there is a bloody maw dripping gore and viscera with a torn intestine dangling from it's teeth.

I blink and the image is gone, leaving only the smooth porcelain skin and ethereal smile hidden just below the top wings.

My fingers twitch at my side.

Two wings splay out behind the Angel's brilliant body, suspending it in the air. The air is stolen from my lungs as I take in the sheer amount of Eyes that adorn the feathers of these wings. They are littered with the slimy organs that have been haunting me and all of them turn to observe me. One moment They look like a pattern on a feather, not dissimilar to the way a peacock's feathers look. The next, my stomach turns and I gag. The image of those Eyes weeping blood as They are splattered like oversized gushers catches me off guard.

I want to—no, I *need* to scream. I need to leave, turn around and never return. But then the image is gone, replaced with the angelic eyed feathers. Innocent patterned feathers that should not scare me, but they do.

My wrist rotates and I poise it to reach into my pocket.

The final two wings hang from the body elegantly—*dangling, broken, bloody*—crossing before what can only be the feet of the Angel. The overlapping images no longer fade in and out, but stutter and flash before me. My nausea ramps up as they do. One moment the Angel is pristine white and gold, the wings neatly crossed before it; the next they are broken and limp, tattered and bloodied as they hang down next to clawed... I can't describe the appendages, they are beyond what I can comprehend.

Too much, this is too much. I can't take it. My eyes slowly travel back up the luminous body. I flinch every time the image shifts, only to continue following the dips and shadows when the holy visage returns.

I have been searching for this Angel my entire life; been shuttered from my church for asking about it, spent countless hours in therapy talking about it, dreamt about it, searched the knowledge of the ancients for years in a cramped study room for it. And now it's here. Floating in front of me.

My swollen knuckles get caught on the edge of my pocket, but with a little fenangling, I'm able to wrap my fingers around the switchblade hidden there. The image shifts once again and my eyes lock on the bloody entrails hanging from the Angel's maw. Every inch of my being—*my hand, my breath, my very consciousness*—comes to a still.

My lungs burn with the held breath, and I nearly cry in relief when the holy purity returns. My arm moves then, pulling the meager blade out of my pocket and flicking it open. I am not sure what I am going to do with it, but I need to do something. Surely a mortal blade like this will do no harm to a heavenly being—

My thought is cut short as the blood returns and I lock onto the viscera again. Time slows as I watch it drop from the maw.

Too much— I don't want— I can't— I need— I need to leave, I need to leave NOW.

I am going to be sick, my eyes roll back as a wave of nausea grips me. Through the white noise static of the Angel, I can hear the viscera as it splashes onto the hardwood of the church floor. I retch, my gaze remaining unfocused as I tell myself that I never want to see such a vile thing again.

I am in pain again. Why? It's nearly unbearable, nearly as mad as seeing the Angel itself. Why am I in pain?

Blood wells around my hand and blurs my vision further and I know. A wave of relief rushes through my body as the realization that I will never have to see anything again. And then I feel a *ka-chink* under the blade in my hand. It's stuck, caught in the fissure of my skull behind my eye. I can feel it deep in my senses as I wiggle the blade, trying to free it. It feels good in the worst way, even as my stomach rolls with another round of nausea.

I yank the blade harder, desperate now in my attempts to free it. But my hands keep slipping, the blood making the hilt too slippery. I need the relief it brought, I need to finish what I started. The Angel, it's still watching, I can still see it. It's smiling down at me with perfect teeth—no, with vicious eyes and a bloody maw—no, with—

Fuck. Bile rises in my throat as I let go of the switchblade, making a last-ditch decision to use my bare hands instead.

My movements are hesitant at first, my fingertips tearing through my eyelid as they press into the space between my skull and my eyeball. A moment of regret, a fleeting thing, as I register just how disgustingly slimy and squishy the organ is. The feeling doesn't last, though, as my need for relief surmounts any other feelings and I push further and further into the socket. My fingers scoop around the orbital nerve, curling around the soft organ and yanking it out of my head.

I drop it to the ground, listening for it to hit the wood floor before softly tapping my boot out in front of me until I locate it. The obscene noise it makes when I squish it beneath my boot makes me groan. It's the sweetest sound I've ever heard.

Complete and utter darkness blesses me. The only blessing I have ever and will ever receive.

I can no longer see, but I can finally breathe again. I know the Angel is still there, I can feel the heat radiating off of it. It's visage is seared into my very being. I know it's there.

I know, but there is nothing I can do as the wail of sirens pierce the air. The air that has become thick with my now silent screams, the viscous blood running down the sides of my face blocking the noise. I can do nothing but fall to my knees on the wet wood of the church floor as I bleed in front of the Angel.

Is this what we consider Holy? Is this what we have spent so much time trying to find? What we hope and pray to see when we die?

Not me. Not now.

My life changed when I heard those three words, and never again shall I search for what they mean.

ACKNOWLEDGEMENTS

Happy birthday, Max! I hope this present helps brightens your day a bit, just like you brighten my day by being my friend!

A special thank you to everyone who made this story happen: Cryptic for giving me the title and therefore the idea for the story, the Shit Show for dealing with my mentally ill rambling about angels and eyes, Xochi for letting me talk about the story even though you don't like horror, Alex for your invaluable feedback when I was stuck on what direction I wanted to go with the story, and my betas for becoming temporary alpha readers in an attempt to help.

I love and appreciate every single one of you. Especially those of you who said that the story could be grosser. Your input made a world of difference.

ABOUT THE AUTHOR

Andromeda Ruins (he/him) is a queer punk from the Middle of Nowhere, Ohio. He recently graduated from his undergraduate program and intends on going to grad school to study with a hopeful Classics major and Folklore studies concentration. Andromeda works full time as well, having gotten himself into a career where he looks at telephone poles all day and makes sure they follow safety criteria set forward by the government.

In his free time Andromeda reads books in dead languages, explores the haunted forests that surround him, and writes. He is queer, disabled, and neurodivergent, sitting comfortably in the 'I don't know what's going on' category in just about everything. This leads to him writing a lot about fucked up queer, disabled, and neurodivergent characters.

ALSO BY ANDROMEDA

<u>Call Me Icarus</u>

Δάιος

χεῖμα

<u>Grief Short Stories</u>

Death Comes For Us All

Wait For Me

Sunburn

<u>Soon To Come</u>

Desecrate (Mar. 2025)